All Ladybird books are available at most bookshops, supermarkets and newsagents, or can be ordered direct from:
Ladybird Postal Sales PO Box 133 Paignton TQ3 2YP England
Telephone: (+44) 01803 554761 *Fax:* (+44) 01803 663394

A catalogue record for this book is available from the British Library

Published by Ladybird Books Ltd
A subsidiary of the Penguin Group
A Pearson Company
LADYBIRD and the device of a Ladybird are trademarks of Ladybird Books Ltd Loughborough Leicestershire UK

Printed and bound in Great Britain by
Butler & Tanner Ltd, Frome and London

DISNEP · PIXAR

a bug's life

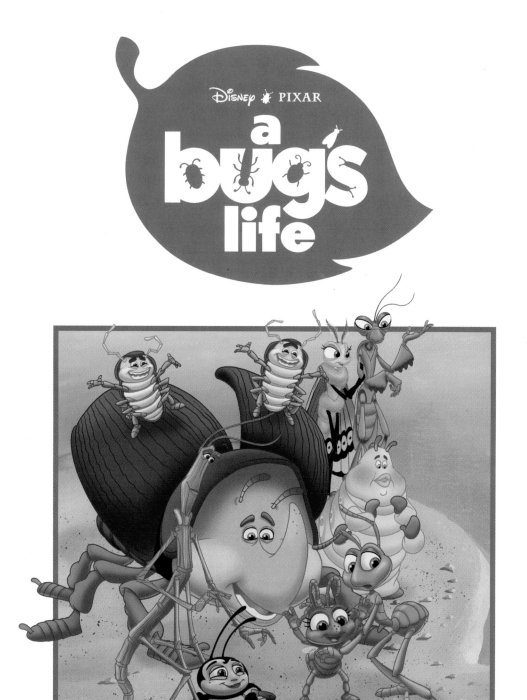

TED SMART

Hidden deep among the grass, Ant Island buzzed with activity as worker ants collected the annual wheat harvest and piled it onto a big stone.

"The grasshoppers will be here soon," said Princess Atta. "Will we have enough food for the offering?" It was Atta's first year in charge of the harvest. She was learning to take over from her mother, the queen. Suddenly, a huge wheat stalk toppled onto the princess.

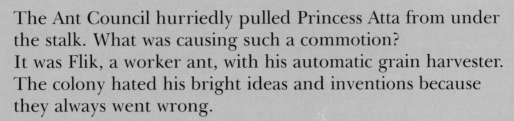

The Ant Council hurriedly pulled Princess Atta from under the stalk. What was causing such a commotion?
It was Flik, a worker ant, with his automatic grain harvester. The colony hated his bright ideas and inventions because they always went wrong.

"You're weird!" laughed Atta's little sister Dot. But she liked Flik. He was kind to Dot and he reassured her when she felt sad about being too little to fly.

Suddenly the colony alarm blared. Flik looked up at the sky. "They're here!" he cried.

Thousands of screaming ants ran in all directions. Giving a shrill whistle, the queen brought the colony to order. The ants hurriedly piled the last of the grain onto the big stone and marched into the anthill. Soon they were all safely underground. But one ant was missing...

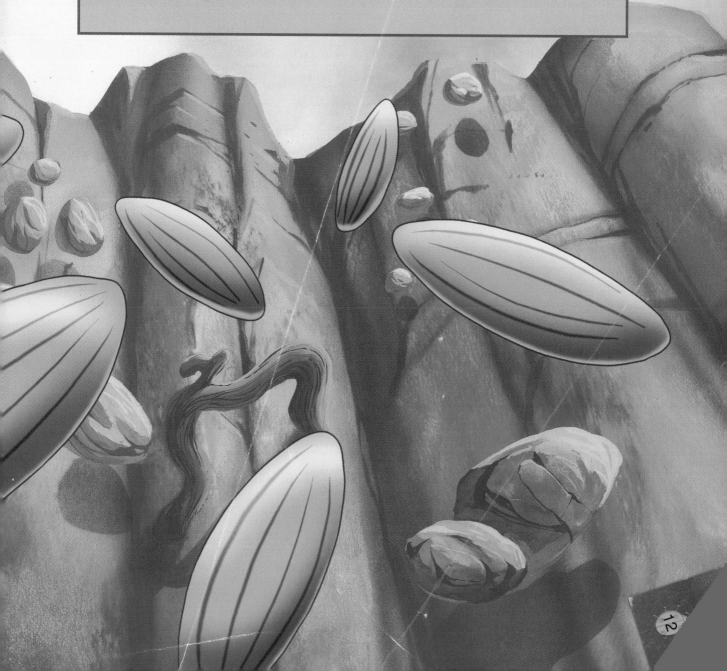

Flik was trying to get out of his grain harvester. He scrambled out and ran. But the machine knocked over the stone that held the grasshoppers' food, spilling the grain into the riverbed.

Flik tried to explain what had happened, but Princess Atta only heard the terrible noise overhead. Suddenly the buzzing stopped.

CRASH! Huge grasshoppers plunged into the anthill.

"Where's my food?" roared Hopper, the leader. Only now did Atta guess what Flik had done! She watched helplessly as the grasshoppers tossed ants into the air. Hopper yelled, "It seems to me you're forgetting your place. So let's double the order of food."

Then Hopper and his gang left, promising to return when the last leaf had fallen.

Flik volunteered to search for bigger bugs to help fight the grasshoppers, but the Ant Council laughed.

"Your search could take weeks!" said Atta.

"Weeks?" everyone echoed. At least Flik would be out of their way. So they sent the worker ant to find some warrior bugs to help the colony.

Meanwhile, in the city, P. T. Flea's circus was doing its best to entertain an audience of flies. Rosie the spider and Dim the giant beetle were booed off the stage. Then the clowns – Francis the ladybird, Slim the stick insect and Heimlich the caterpillar got into an argument with some flies! Even Manny the mantis couldn't rescue the performance with his magic act.

There was only one thing left...

"Flaming Death!" screamed P. T. "I hold in my hand the match that decides whether two bugs live or die this very evening!"

As a trail of matches leading to a sheet of flypaper was set alight, Tuck and Roll the pill bug cannonballs, prepared to be fired. But everything went wrong—it was P. T. who flew towards the flypaper!

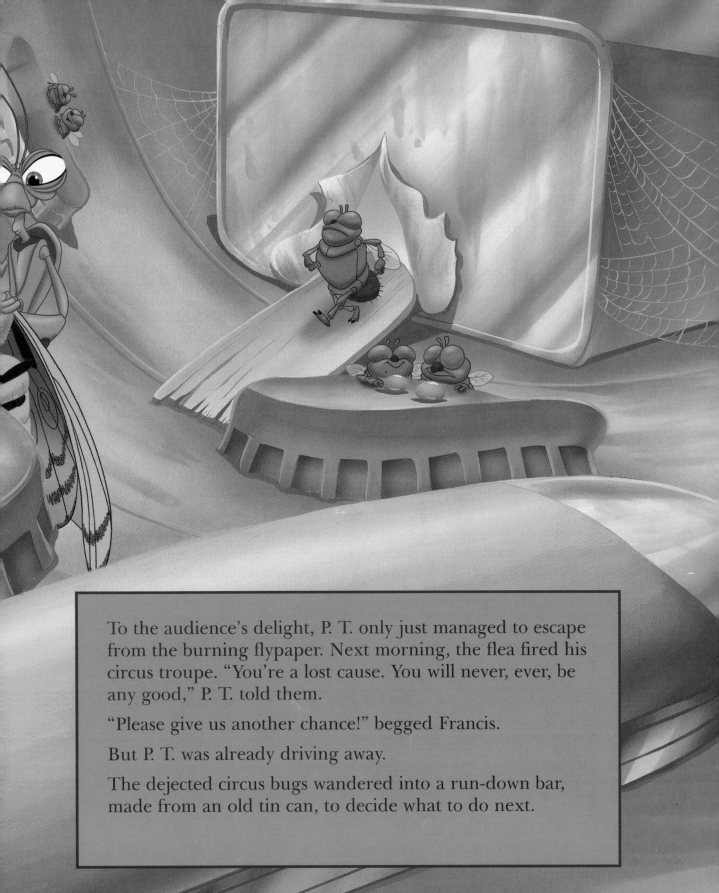

To the audience's delight, P. T. only just managed to escape from the burning flypaper. Next morning, the flea fired his circus troupe. "You're a lost cause. You will never, ever, be any good," P. T. told them.

"Please give us another chance!" begged Francis.

But P. T. was already driving away.

The dejected circus bugs wandered into a run-down bar, made from an old tin can, to decide what to do next.

The circus bugs were soon in trouble again. The flies Francis had argued with the night before appeared, looking for a fight. Francis and Slim shouted, "Stand back! We are the greatest warriors in the land!" At that moment Flik walked into the bar and heard the word 'warriors'. His search for help was over!

But the fight was getting out of hand and the circus bugs ran. The bar tipped over and tossed everyone into the air. The circus bugs landed on top of the flies.

Flik thought they'd won. "I've been searching all over for bugs with your talent!" he grinned.

Thinking Flik was a talent scout, the circus bugs flew back to Ant Island with him. Flik tried to tell them about Hopper and his gang, but the sound of Dim's wings drowned out his voice.

The ant colony looked terrified when they saw the circus bugs and Francis thought they were going to send them away. "We guarantee a performance like no other!" he said quickly. "When the grasshoppers arrive, we'll knock 'em dead!"

Later the ants held a banquet to celebrate the 'warrior' bugs' arrival. Then Rosie and her friends watched as young ants performed a play showing how the brave bugs would die – fighting the grasshoppers. Only now, as Princess Atta thanked the warriors for helping them, did the circus bugs understand why they were really there. They pulled Flik to one side to tell him the truth.

"What made you think we were warriors?" gasped Rosie.

"You ran around that bar knocking over customers like they were flies!" whispered Flik.

"They *were* flies!" said Francis.

The bugs started to leave, but Flik wasn't going to give up. Flik chased after the bugs, yelling, "You can't leave, you've got to help me!"

But before the circus bugs could reply, Flik screamed "Run!"
A huge, hungry sparrow was flying towards them!

Dot had seen Flik leave, and wanted to know what was going
on. But she was too young to be able to fly. Dot grabbed a
dandelion seed and floated down.

"Don't leave, Flik!" she called. Hearing Dot shout, the massive
bird let out a piercing screech – and swooped towards her.

Dot let go of the dandelion seed just before the bird's great beak snapped shut. Luckily, Francis caught Dot inches above the ground. Stumbling backwards, Francis and Dot fell into a crack in the riverbed. Francis's leg was pinned under a big rock, and it was Dot's turn to help Francis. While she tried to free Francis's leg, Heimlich and Slim distracted the bird.

Meanwhile, Flik and the other circus bugs went to rescue Dot and Francis. Rosie the spider used a web to lower Flik, Tuck and Roll into the crack. The three insects lifted Francis and Dot into the web and Dim flew his friends to the safety of a thorn bush. The bird couldn't reach them there!

Suddenly the bugs heard a strange sound. "What's that noise?" asked Rosie.

"That, my friends, is the sound of applause," said Manny. Peering down, they were amazed to see cheering ants. The bugs were heroes!

"I'm sorry I doubted you, Flik," Atta smiled. "Sometimes I feel like the whole colony is watching me, waiting for me to..."

"Make a mistake?" said Flik.

The princess suddenly understood how Flik always felt.

"I thought you'd hired a bunch of clowns. But they were so brave!" said Atta. "Not everyone would face a big bird. Even Hopper's afraid of them."

That gave Flik another idea. They could build a mechanical bird to scare Hopper! Knowing the Ant Council wouldn't listen to anything he said, Flik asked Manny to pretend he'd thought of the idea. The Ant Council loved Manny's plan, and work on the bird began.

Using nutshells, acorns, leaves and twigs, the ants made a hollow bird. Rosie's spider silk held the frame together. Then leaves were added to look like feathers.

After helping the ants to build a launch platform, they raised the bird high above the anthill.

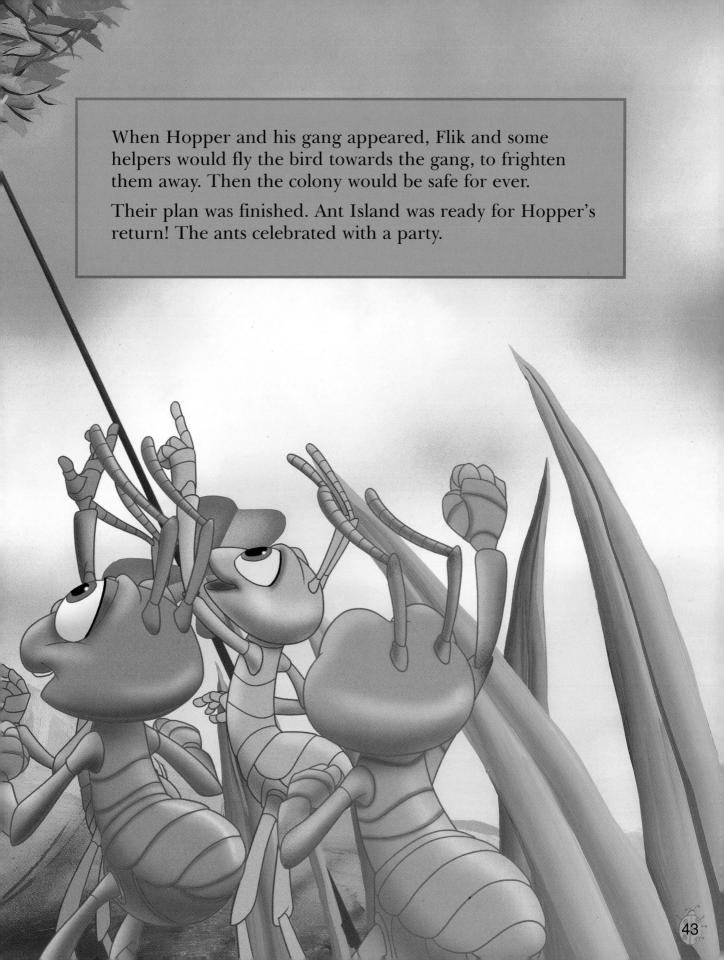

When Hopper and his gang appeared, Flik and some helpers would fly the bird towards the gang, to frighten them away. Then the colony would be safe for ever.

Their plan was finished. Ant Island was ready for Hopper's return! The ants celebrated with a party.

Far away, in their desert hide-out, the lazy grasshoppers were relaxing. Molt asked Hopper why they needed to go back to the ant colony.

A light blazed in Hopper's good eye. "Those ants outnumber us a hundred to one!" he roared. "It's not about food, it's about keeping the ants in line! Now let's ride!"

Back at the colony, things were going well until P. T. Flea arrived. He had been searching for his circus bugs, and showed the ants a poster of his troupe. When the ants recognised the circus bugs, they realised their brave 'warriors' were really clowns!

"But the bird will still work!" Flik insisted. Atta was too angry to listen to him.

Atta and the queen were worried. Hopper would arrive soon, and they hadn't collected enough food! The queen ordered the circus bugs to leave. Atta told Flik to go with them.

Only Princess Dot was sad to see Flik leave. She tried to follow him, but the queen held her back. The rest of the ants were too busy watching the last leaf flutter to the ground.

But before the ants could decide what to do next, the grasshoppers arrived. When Hopper saw the tiny pile of grain waiting for him, he was furious.

Atta tried to explain, but Hopper pushed her away and grabbed the queen. "No ant sleeps until we get every scrap of food," he snarled.

Then he ordered his gang to raid the colony's storerooms.

Dot knew she had to find Flik. She flapped her little wings as hard as she could and suddenly she was flying! Spotting P. T.'s wagon, she rushed to tell them what had happened.

"The grasshoppers have taken our food—and they're going to squish my mum!" Dot gasped.

Flik and the circus bugs hurried back to Ant Island. There they put on a show to distract the grasshoppers, who were munching their way through the ants' food.

Whilst Manny and Gypsy performed their magic act, Flik quietly climbed into the mechanical bird. The bird swooped towards the grasshoppers, who all ran for cover.

But P. T. didn't know anything about Flik's plan and he rushed to protect the circus bugs from the 'bird'. Crying, "Flaming Death!" he set it on fire! Flik's plan had failed – and Hopper realised he'd been tricked.

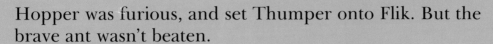

Hopper was furious, and set Thumper onto Flik. But the brave ant wasn't beaten.

"Somehow, every year, ants pick food for themselves and for you. Who's the weaker species?" gasped Flik. Hopper lunged at Flik, who ran to the edge of Ant Island and backed towards the sparrows nest. Hopper followed. The last thing he saw was a huge bird beak closing around him. Hopper was gone for ever!

Soon it was spring on Ant Island. P. T. Flea and his circus troupe were saying their goodbyes. Atta adjusted her crown—she was now in charge and the queen had retired. Flik was the colony's official inventor. Thanks to his bravery the colony would never be bothered by Hopper again.